TÍA ISA
WANTS A CAR

TÍA ISA
WANTS A CAR

Meg Medina

illustrated by **Claudio Muñoz**

CANDLEWICK PRESS

*T*ía Isa wants a car.

She tells me after work when she still smells of lemon pies from the bakery.

She is turning the jump rope that's tied to the fence, and I am already up to twenty.

"Un pisicorre," she says, "to take us to the beach!"

"Really? The beach?" I can't catch my breath.

No one goes far from my block in the summer. But a beach has foamy water that reaches all the places I cannot go.

"Sí, really. Let's save."

Tía Isa wants a car.

"What color?" I ask as we climb the steps to our apartment, past our neighbors' doors. From under the cracks, I hear the scrape of forks and smell the boiled hot dogs on their tables.

"The same shiny green as the ocean that lapped outside my bedroom window," she says. When Tía Isa was a girl, the air on her island smelled of wet palm fronds and mud.

"And pointy wings off the back!" I say.
"When we go fast, we'll look like the gulls
that swooped for your crab buckets."
It's my favorite Tía story.
"Yes," she says. "Así."

Tía Isa wants a car.

But Tío Andrés laughs when he hears his sister's plan.

"Don't be ridiculous!" he says. "You're not a rich queen! We walk to everything we need here, Isa. Now, what's for dinner?"

Tía Isa just whistles as she steps over Tío's work boots— muddy like ogre shoes—and stirs our black-bean soup.

Later that night, Tía Isa takes out the fat money envelope from her drawer in our room.

"Two piles," she says.

I make a stack, tall and straight. That's our helping money, which we will send back home—along with notes and pictures so Mami can see how I've grown.

What's left is for Tía Isa's car. *Too little*, I think, *not as tall as a pinch*.

But Tía Isa only crosses her arms.

"What did that bossy brother of mine say?" she asks.

"He said, 'Rrrridículo,'" I repeat with Tío's hard *r*'s, like a cat purring.

"We'll see about that," she says.

Tía Isa wants a car.

Is it waiting for us inside this lot that smells of tar? We walk along, sucking on red Popsicles and looking at the clouds reflected on the glassy hoods.

"How much, mister? How much?" Tía Isa repeats in the few English words she knows. She shows him her envelope.

"Not enough," the man tells us again, shaking his head.

"We'll have the money soon," Tía Isa says as we wait for the bus.

But *soon* is when our family is going to join us here, so I know *soon* can be a very long time.

"Tía Isa wants a car. But we don't have enough," I tell Señor Leo, who is sweeping his fruit store.

He stops to scratch his shiny head and has an idea.

"Help me stack those oranges nice and pretty, niña, and I'll pay you."

"Tía Isa wants a car," I tell la vieja María, who has windowsill cats but can't bend her creaky back to feed them.

She looks over her dusty glasses and holds out her extra key.

"Come after school, mi vida, to give the kittens milk. I'll pay you."

"Tía Isa wants a car," I tell Miss Amy, who speaks no Spanish but wants to invite Señor Pérez over for ham sandwiches. How will they tell each other good stories? "Teach me some español," she begs. "I'll pay you."

Tía Isa wants a car.

But why does it take so long to save?

"Sometimes it's hard to wait for good things to happen," she says.

Then she reads me Mami's letter. Abuelo is feeling a little better. Mami feeds him crab soup. Papi plays him old songs on his guitar.

So I wait and wait until one day my secret money sock has grown into a giant money sausage and can't wait anymore.

I show Tía my surprise. The curly bills tumble onto her bed.
She leaves two pink lip marks on my forehead from her besito.

"Vamos, Tía, let's go," I tell her, tiptoeing past Tío Andrés, who is playing cards with the men from work. She chases after me all the way to the lot.

Tía Isa wants a car.

And I find it.

Hiding near the rusty fence.

Shiny green.

Wide as the porch of Tía Isa's old house.

Already I can feel the seashells between my toes.

"Ese mismo," she says. The very one.

"Bad radio. No air conditioning," warns the man.

But Tía Isa is already touching the front seat, big enough for three. She nods when I show her there's room in the back for more of us, who'll come soon.

"You're right, mi hija," she says. "This one will take us all where we want to go."

"We'll take it!" I tell the man.

Tía Isa turns on the car, whose motor cranks with a puff of genie smoke, and then it says, *Arroz, arroz, arroz, arroz.*

"First things first," she says.

She pulls out the only thing left in our envelope, which is skinny now like an empty balloon.

It's a picture of our whole family. Me, Tía Isa, and Tío Andrés. But also my parents, grandparents, and cousins—los padres, abuelos, and primos—who are still there, thinking about us from that breezy house by the sea.

I hold the picture steady while she tapes down the corners.

Then Tía Isa leans into the Hula-hoop wheel, and off we go!

My ponytail flaps behind me like a rope cut loose. We zoom along Sanford Avenue, past my school and the other buildings, so squat and red. Past a bus full of tired people squeezed close the way I hate, with no room to spin around on the bars inside.

"Tía Isa bought a car!" I shout.

KEEP OFF

Tía Isa steers us to the spot I point to. The rumbling car fits in the space just right. Our neighbors come out to see.

"Hurry now. Apúrate," she tells me.

I check for the frowning super and run to the patch of Keep Off grass. I whistle until Tío Andrés finally comes out to look.

"Tía Isa bought a car!" I call. "Come down and see!"

He laughs in surprise at his *rrrr*idiculous sister.

"You did it!" he says, smiling to his back teeth.

"*We* did it," Tía Isa says. "And there's room for us all."

Tía Isa and I bought a car.
To carry us all to the sea.

For the real Tía Isa—Ysaira Metauten.
And in memory of Tía Gera—Gerardina Metauten.
M. M.

To my dearest granddaughter, Lili, her own Tía Isa,
and my beloved sister Anandy.
C. M.

Text copyright © 2011 by Margaret Medina
Illustrations copyright © 2011 by Claudio Muñoz

First paperback edition 2016

Library of Congress Catalog Card Number 2010040128
ISBN 978-0-7636-4156-6 (hardcover)
ISBN 978-0-7636-5752-9 (paperback)

21 22 23 24 APS 13 12

Printed in Humen, Dongguan, China

This book was typeset in Maiandra.
The illustrations were done in pencil, watercolor, and ink.

Candlewick Press
99 Dover Street
Somerville, Massachusetts 02144

visit us at www.candlewick.com